To Sophie, who gave me the idea for this book when she was very little. And to Maia, Sophie, and Livia, who made the animal drawings. To each of you—my thanks and my love —N.P.

To M.E.B., S.L.B., and L.C.B., with my love and appreciation, too —S.L.R.

KIMCHEE (or kimchi) is the national dish of Korea—a highly seasoned mixture of pickled cabbage, onions, and sometimes fish. Green beans, bean sprouts, and large white radishes may also be added. Red hot peppers, garlic, ginger, and horseradish are combined in various ways to create kimchee. Several different versions of this spicy dish may be served at a Korean meal.

Typeset in Highlander • Art created using collage, ink drawings, and oil pastels

Published by Bloomsbury Publishing, New York, London, and Berlin
Distributed to the trade by Holtzbrinck Publishers

Library of Congress Cataloging-in-Publication Data
Patz, Nancy.
Babies can't eat kimchee! / by Nancy Patz and Susan L. Roth.—1st U.S. ed.
p. cm.
Summary: A baby sister must wait to grow up before doing big sister things, such as eating spicy Korean food and ballet dancing.
ISBN-10: 1-59990-017-3 • ISBN-13: 978-1-59990-017-9
[1. Babies—Fiction. 2. Sisters—Fiction. 3. Growth—Fiction. 4. Korean Americans—Fiction.] I. Roth, Susan L. II. Title. III. Title: Babies cannot eat kimchee!
PZ7.P27833Bab 2007 [E]—dc22 2006006942

First U.S. Edition 2007
Printed in Singapore
10 9 8 7 6 5 4 3 2 1

Bloomsbury Publishing, Children's Books, U.S.A.
175 Fifth Avenue, New York, NY 10010

All papers used by Bloomsbury Publishing are natural, recyclable products made from wood grown in well-managed forests. The manufacturing processes conform to the environmental regulations of the country of origin.

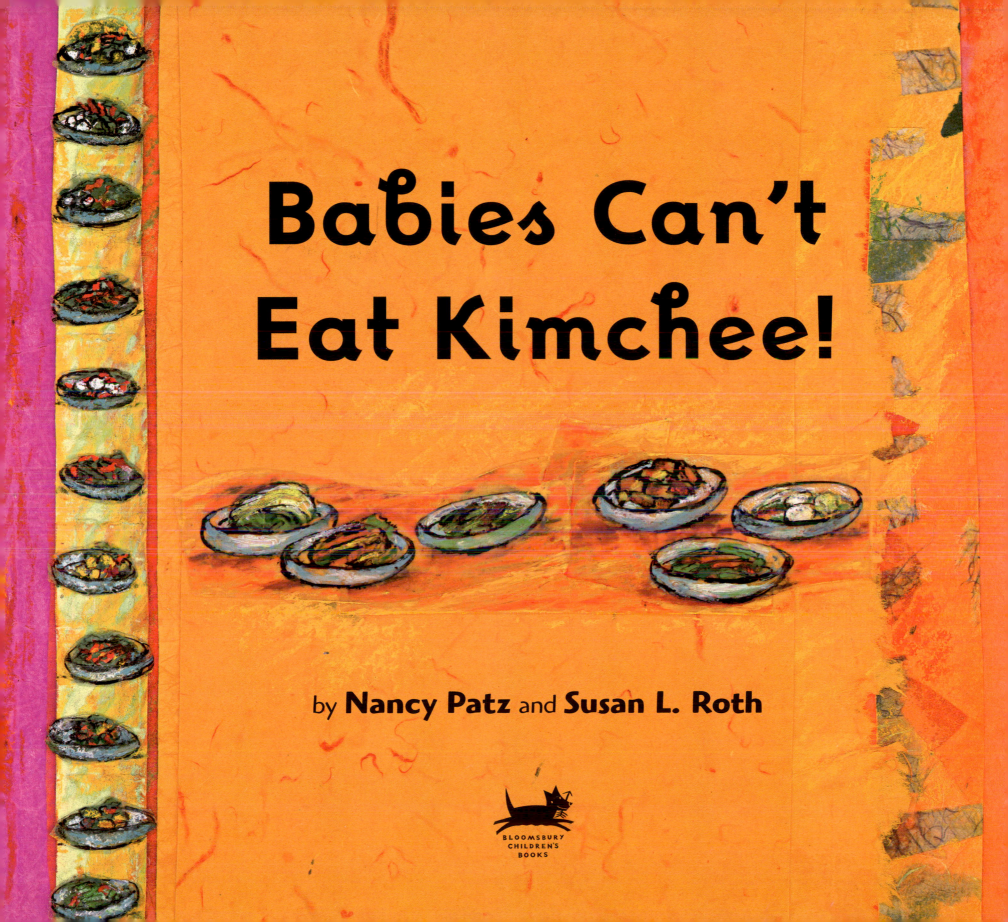

Babies Can't
Eat Kimchee!

by **Nancy Patz** and **Susan L. Roth**

BLOOMSBURY
CHILDREN'S
BOOKS

Babies can't eat kimchee!

And they can't
eat spaghetti.
Or popcorn.
And they can't
eat strawberry
ice cream cones,
the way I can.

Babies can't eat
lots of things.

They don't
know how
to dance
like a ballerina,
the way I do.

And they can't
wear big girl
dress-up clothes.

They don't even
know what an
elephant is.

Or a tiger.

Or a duck.

And babies don't

know that a snake

says, *"Hiss . . ."*

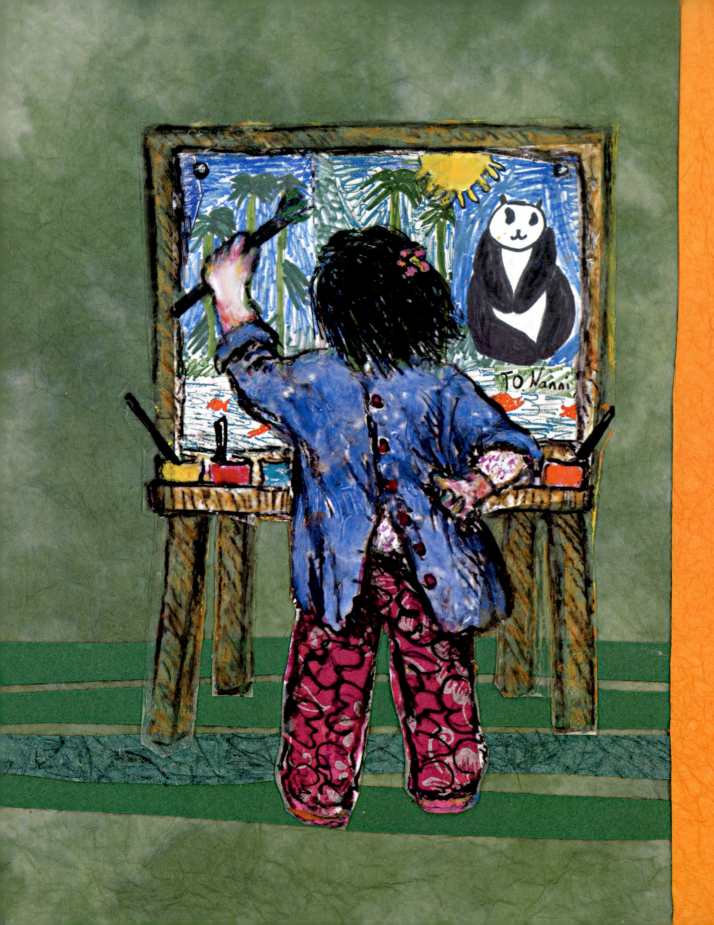

Babies don't know lots of things. They don't know their colors. They won't wear their smocks.

And sometimes they make a BIG FUSS!

Because they're very little.

But babies get bigger. Then I'll teach this baby to walk. And look both ways at the corner. When we have ice cream, I'll teach her how to lick up the drips.

And on her
first birthday,
I'll help her
put on her
special dress.

I'll teach my baby to dance

like a ballerina.

We'll swing high!

And do you know
what else?

Early in the
morning when
everybody's sleeping,

we'll whisper and
read funny stories
and play with our
toys and laugh.
And eat kimchee,
if we want to.

Baby, do you
want me to teach
you a song?

Well, maybe someday . . .